LADY BIRD

MY EIGHT LIVES

Carolyn Crampton

*Dedicated to those who make
life better for other creatures.*

CHAPTER 1

I'm a bunny called Ladybird.
Maybe I'll tell you my tale.

I once lived with my mother and siblings,
Both female and male.

We lived at a bunny home,
Nuzzling our bunny mother.

She groomed us every day,
One after another.

CHAPTER
2

Too soon, hands snatched us from Mom,
And moved us to a store.

I did not know then,
I wouldn't see her anymore.

One bunny day, hands put me in a box.
I was so very small.

The box shook back and forth.
I rolled around like a ball.

CHAPTER
3
SNOWBALL

The jostling stopped. Smaller hands lifted me.
I met a boy and girl.

They picked me up too high,
And spun me around with a whirl.

I tumbled to the ground,
Paws over ears.

I hid under the bed,
Frightened, hiding tears.

While the children rested,
I nibbled on their lunch.

I found a leafy toy, so good,
To rip and munch.

But my exploration often caused,
A most alarming yell.

One day, a beast came to stay,
With a rotten smell.

With huge teeth and raucous barking,
He began a chase.

The beast tried to reach me,
In my hiding place.

25

CHAPTER 4

From that day, I lived in a cage,
With no chance to run.

I heard the children laughing outside,
In the sun.

29

Left alone, for a very long time,
I had nothing to do.

When stuffed in a box, I tried to escape.
But my attempt fell through.

The box rocked and swayed.
I was overcome with fright.

Until, a new boy gently lifted me,
And hugged me warm and tight.

CHAPTER 5
THUMPER

He housed me in a wire hutch,
High off the ground.

Each afternoon, he let me out,
To dig, and hop around.

But I passed time alone,
While the sky was light.

And I was always left alone,
To make it through the night.

When it was cold, hungry creatures came,
To scratch and to claw.

When it was warm, a mouse squeezed inside,
To nibble and to gnaw.

One day, the boy kissed my head.
Then, he sped away.

His mother would bring me water
And feed me every day.

I lunged for a carrot,
But bit her finger by mistake.

She screamed. I hopped out,
And made my escape.

CHAPTER 6

STRAY A80384

I ran wildly until dark,
Aching all over, but on I kept.

I collapsed under a hedge.
Wild animals awoke and crept.

At dawn, two runners spied me,
Then, jogged off down the street.

A man crawled up near me,
Offering a tasty treat.

Trapped again,
So soon! For want of a meal.

I was placed across from others,
In a buzzing room of steel.

A woman came close,
With sweet, soothing words to say.

Then, she opened my cage,
And carried me away.

CHAPTER
7
LUCY

She gently probed and checked me.
She held me warm and close.

Tucked beneath her arm,
She trimmed my toes.

My new home was quite spacious.
A neighborly place to stay.

Children came to hold bunnies,
And to take them away.

Several seasons calmly passed,
When suddenly, inside my crate…

Appeared a small, white bunny,
A new roommate.

At first,
I resented the intruder.

But soon, he became
My snuggle brother.

A new woman talked to me softly,
Face-to-face.

Before long, my brother and I,
Moved to another place.

Frightened by the vehicle's motion,
I squeezed into my brother's box to hide.

She invited me to exit,
After a bumpy ride.

CHAPTER
8
LADYBIRD

My bunny brother and I romped all over,
Free to roam.

Could this finally be,
A safe, loving home?

We each had a box,
(Though we liked to trade).

My brother and I snuggled.
No longer afraid.

We groomed each other,
And gamboled on the floor.

The lady scritched me tenderly,
(Which I adore).

Once my brother scratched
At a door…

We gained a fresh, green area
To explore.

We lounged in a place,
Not too shady, nor too sunny.

With the woman perched beside us,
Painting—a bunny.

It was me, she painted!
I could hardly believe it.

She depicted me as a smart
And winsome rabbit.

Now, we act as models
(When we choose to pose).

I feel loved and treasured.
Each day the feeling grows.

I learned that life is not always
An enchanted fairytale.

But if you wait—
Love finds us all, without fail.

This is an amalgamation of true stories. Judy at RabbitEars Pet Rescue obtained Ladybird from a public shelter and estimated that Ladybird was three years old. Ladybird lived at RabbitEars for about a year. The author's small, white bunny really did have a play date there to find a companion. Ladybird seems to enjoy posing for the author's paintings.

Thanks to Judy Hardin at RabbitEars. org, the Animal Care Services of Berkeley and San Francisco, and the House Rabbit Society.

Thanks to Lassie, Lucy, Malcolm Little, Ike, Slushie, Ladybird, and Sweatergirl for their love and patience.

A huge thanks to Heidi Goldstein, who wrote the first rhymes and suggested improvements, and to Gabrielle Banks for editorial suggestions.

Thanks to my readers: Karen Crosby-Skilowitz, Jeanne DiGennaro, Kathleen McNamara, and Mary Ann Wolf.

www.ingramcontent.com/pod-product-compliance
Lightning Source LLC
Chambersburg PA
CBHW041640010726
47507CB00011B/415